# The Big BOOK
## for little hands

a book by
Marie-Pascale Cocagne,
Bridget Strevens-Marzo,

### and you:

.............................

Tate Publishing

Make this book your own!
Use your , your ,
your and your .
You can make pictures
any way you want.
It's up to you.
And when you're done,
you can enjoy
the book you've made forever.

# Have fun!

*For Éloïse,*
*who loves letting*
*her crayons loose*
*on pieces of paper.*
M.-P. C.

*For Lucien, Pierre,*
*Samson, Gilles, Keir,*
*Samuel and Oreste,*
*who can be found*
*in the pictures!*
B.

Text: Marie-Pascale Cocagne; illustration: Bridget Strevens-Marzo
English edition first published 2007 by Tate Publishing, Millbank, London SW1P 4RG
www.tate.org.uk/publishing
English language edition © Tate 2007
Reprinted 2008
First published in French as *Les Petits Mains Dessinent*
© Bayard Éditions Jeunesse 2006
All rights reserved.

Thanks to Anna Shandro and Alice Thorp for the English translation

A catalogue record for this book is available from the British Library
ISBN 978-185437-753-1
Distributed in the United States and Canada by Harry N. Abrams, Inc., New York
Library of Congress Control Number: 2006935672

Printed in Malaysia

Draw lots more raindrops.
It will make the frog even happier!

**Can you brighten up
the three bears' house?**

What do you like to eat?
Little Bear is going to treat himself!

The car needs a road
so that Mr Bear can fill up the tank.

Mr Bear is cleaning the car.
Can you help him by using a blue crayon to make all the foam go away?

Do you know what the plants will be?
Draw them in and let us see!

Mrs Bear likes pretty dresses and shoes.
What will she wear today — you choose!

These rabbits are all in white.
Why not dress them up how you like?

Draw some more curly wool
on the back of Mother Sheep and her baby.

Draw the wire around the bales of hay.
That will stop them blowing away!

It's time to feed the hens.
But . . . where have all of their chicks gone?

All of the rabbits love carrots.
Yum, what a treat!

The cow wants more patches, the sheep wants more curls,
and the dog wants more spots.

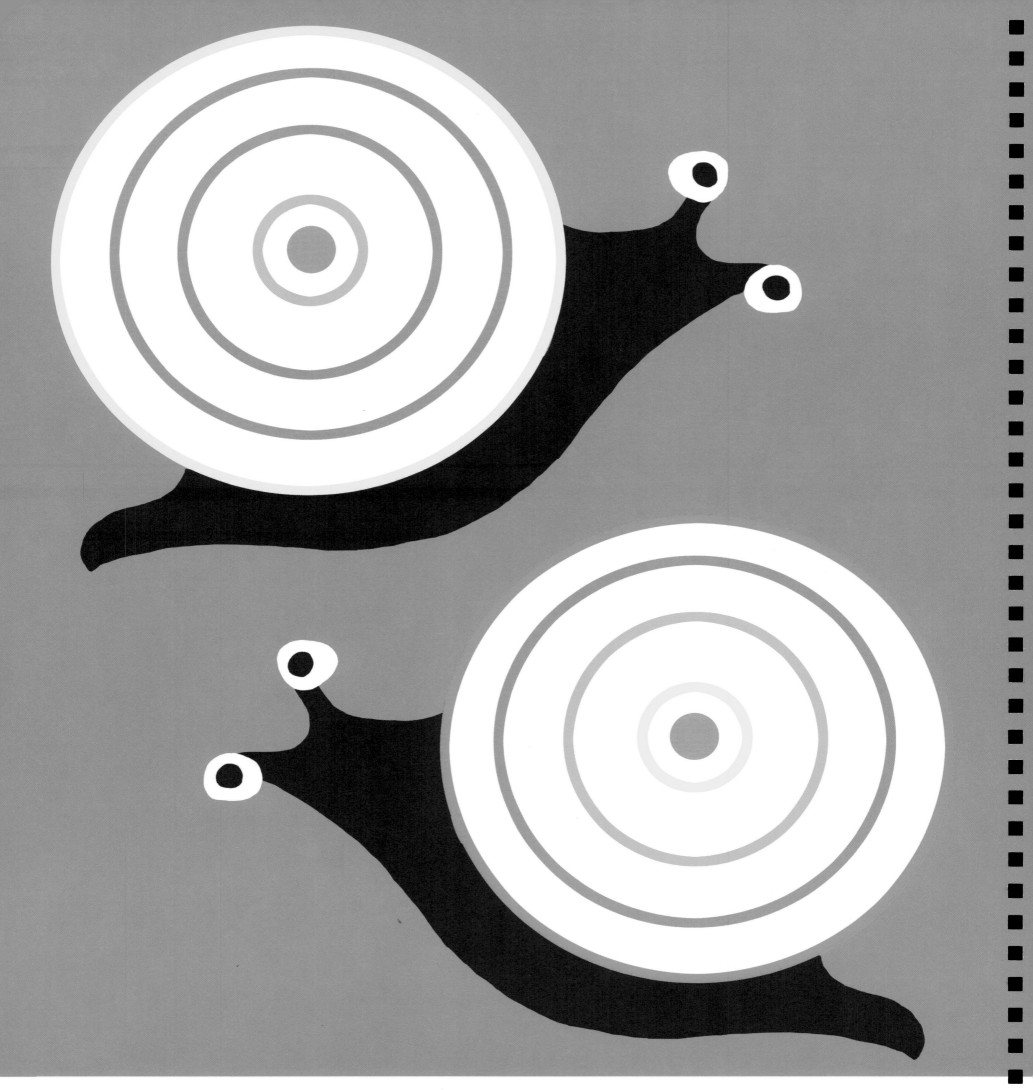

These snails like their shells!

This caterpillar would love to be just as flashy as the snails!

Where are your spots and your beautiful red coats?

Wait a minute little bugs, let's make you even prettier!

These chicks need you to make them complete!

This butterfly would love some party wings to impress its friends.

Three little pigs are waiting for you
to fill their bottles with chocolate milk.

This little girl is spilling her delicious yogurt
all over her bib!

Help the animals walk through the forest.

There is still a lot of work to be done in this little town!

Skipping and jumping is great fun!

This little zebra loves stripes, even on his clothes and bags!

All of the children have to smile for the photo. Say cheese!

Rub with your crayon to make the baby's chickenpox better.

How many candles will there be on your birthday cake?

Red fish, yellow ducks, green turtle . . . Happy fishing, rabbits!

Brighten up the shapes
in the clear blue sky . . .

Hang on, monkeys! You have to put at least four suitcases on the roof of the car before you leave.

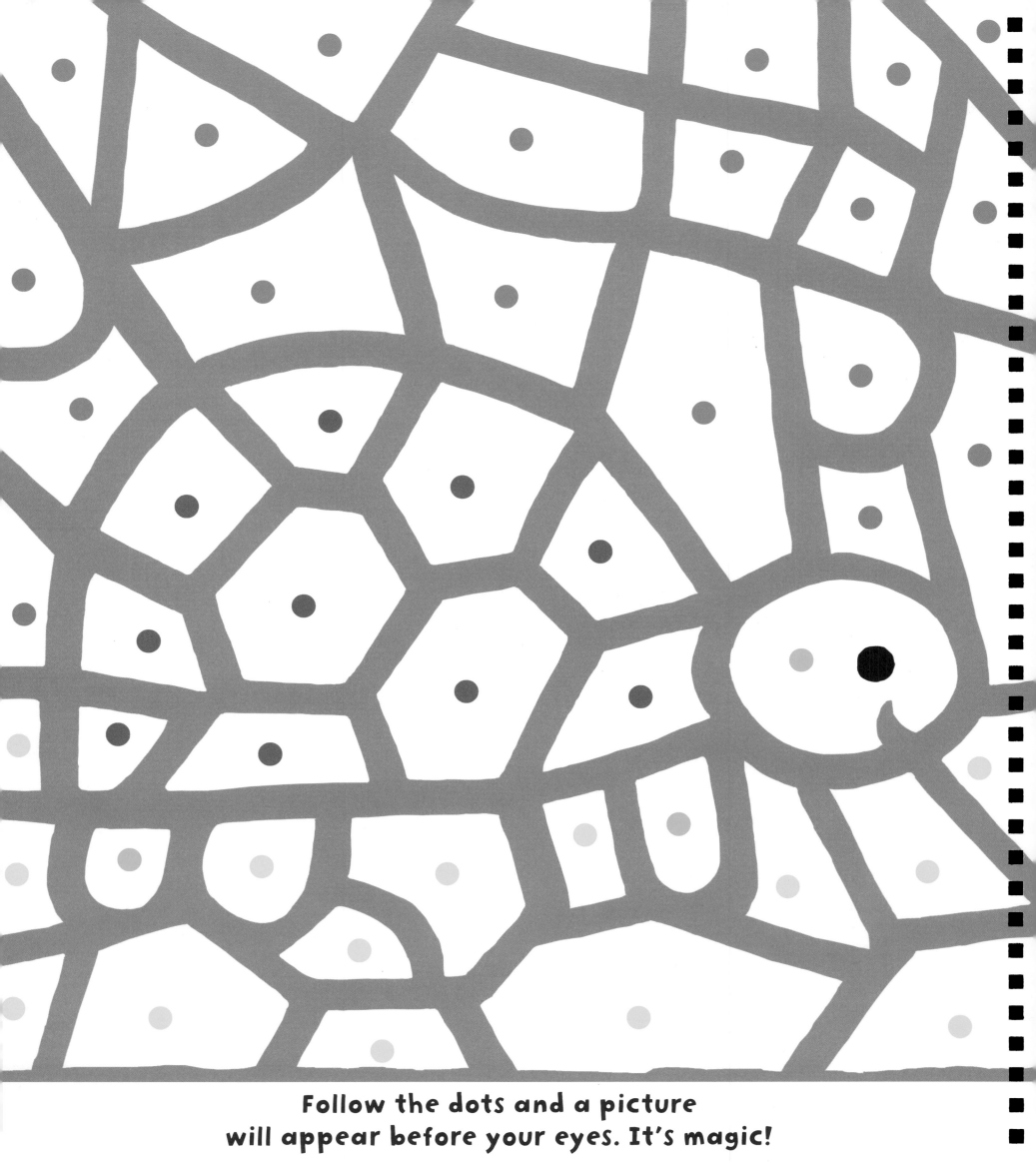

Follow the dots and a picture
will appear before your eyes. It's magic!

Come on little fish,
make some big bubbles like Mother!

These two white octopuses want to be as bright
as their friend. Can you help?

**Follow each white wave with your crayon
until you reach the little fish.**

**Mr Cat hasn't finished
getting dressed yet!**

Wait a moment, little kitten,
someone will make the other shoes just as pretty.

Draw a terrifying monster,
with lots of hair, big teeth and claws.

Draw a kind and gentle monster
with a big smile.

This witch always wants her broomsticks
to look the best. Can you help her?

**Oh no! The witch's spell has gone wrong!**
**What frightening creature is about to crawl out of her cauldron?**

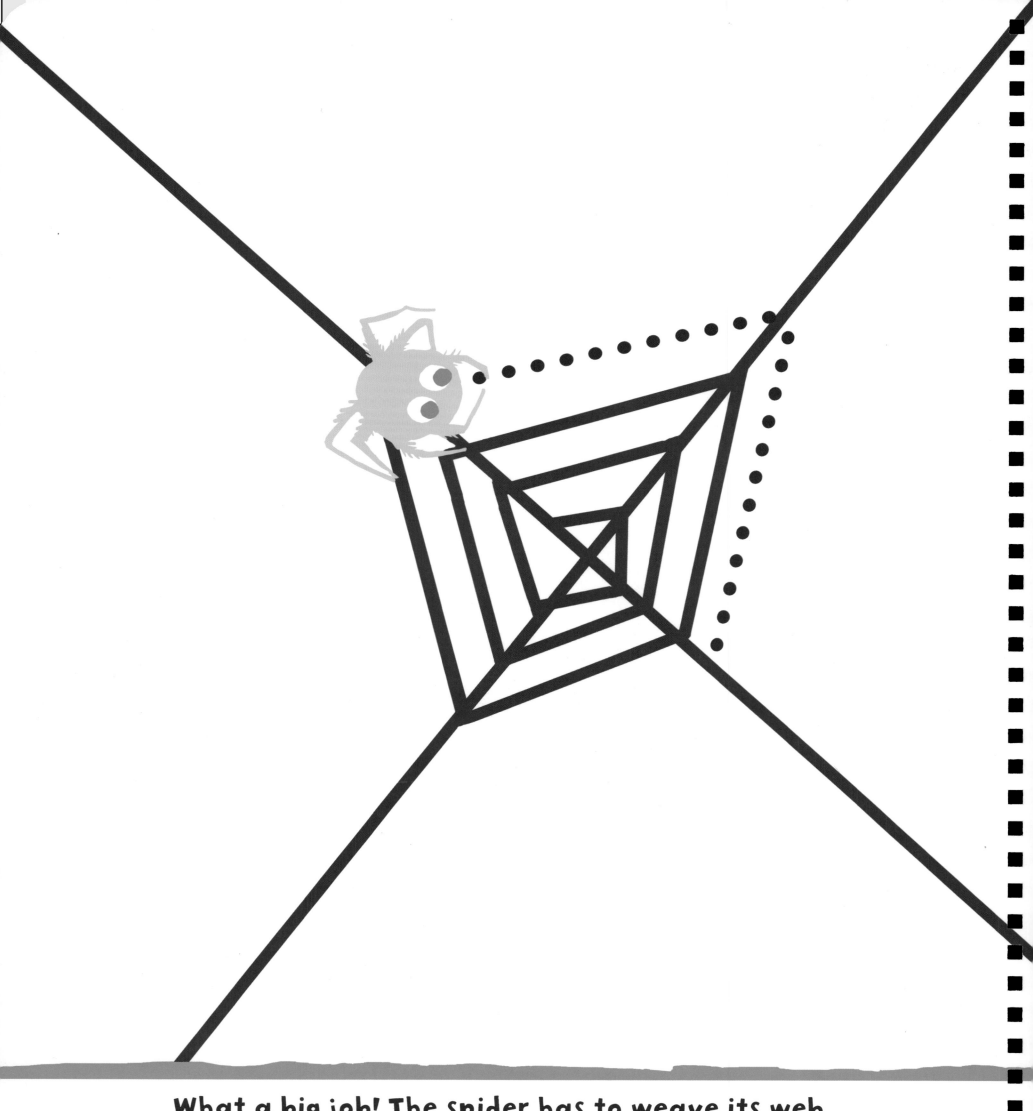

**What a big job! The spider has to weave its web
to fill the whole page!**

A chameleon doesn't like to be seen.
Help this one hide by covering it with green spots.

Lily's hair is too long!
Cut her hair by making the ends red.

Rosie wants lots of hair.
Can you make her dream come true?

Shorten Alice's curls with a dark yellow pen.

Lisa would love to have some beautifully long curls.

Jessica wants pink bows, Phoebe wants orange bows and Anna wants red bows, to match their dresses.

Green hair, long hair, curly hair . . .
anything goes!

**Each seal wants to balance as many balls as possible on its nose. How many can you draw?**

I'm the King of the Jungle!

Every child wants to skip and jump. Can you help?

Help the juggler by making all the balls turn red.

A clown that cries,
a clown that laughs — what fun!

**What a trick to play
on Bozo the clown! It's just as well he has an umbrella.**

Help decorate the Christmas tree.

What are the reindeer going to eat?

How bright the stars are tonight. Can you make them even brighter?
Goodbye little hands!